For Jay – M.B.P.
For Reuben, my dad – R.W.A.

DIAL BOOKS FOR YOUNG READERS
A division of Penguin Young Readers Group • Published by The Penguin Group
Penguin Group (USA) Inc., 375 Hudson Street, New York, NY 10014, U.S.A. • Penguin Group (Canada), 90 Eglinton Avenue East, Suite 700, Toronto, Ontario, Canada M4P 2Y3 (a division of Pearson Penguin Canada Inc.) • Penguin Books Ltd, 80 Strand, London WC2R 0RL, England • Penguin Ireland, 25 St. Stephen's Green, Dublin 2, Ireland (a division of Penguin Books Ltd) • Penguin Group (Australia), 250 Camberwell Road, Camberwell, Victoria 3124, Australia (a division of Pearson Australia Group Pty Ltd) • Penguin Books India Pvt Ltd, 11 Community Centre, Panchsheel Park, New Delhi - 110 017, India • Penguin Group (NZ), 67 Apollo Drive, Rosedale, Auckland 0632, New Zealand (a division of Pearson New Zealand Ltd) • Penguin Books (South Africa) (Pty) Ltd, 24 Sturdee Avenue, Rosebank, Johannesburg 2196, South Africa • Penguin Books Ltd, Registered Offices: 80 Strand, London WC2R 0RL, England

The publisher does not have any control over and does not assume
any responsibility for author or third-party websites or their content.
Text set in Burgstaedt Antiqua Com
Manufactured in China on acid-free paper
10 9 8 7 6 5

     Library of Congress Cataloging-in-Publication Data
 Parker, Marjorie Blain.
   When dads don't grow up / by Marjorie Blain Parker ;
pictures by R.W. Alley.
     p. cm.
   Summary: Extols the virtues of dads who still read comics
and watch cartoons, understand that clothes do not have
to match and that pancakes need not be round, and do not
mind getting their hair wet—if they have any.
   ISBN 978-0-8037-3717-4 (hardcover)
 [1. Fathers—Fiction.] I. Alley, R. W. (Robert W.), ill. II. Title.
III. Title: When dads do not grow up.
   PZ7.P22718Wh 2012
   [E]—dc23
                    2011021628

The art was created using pen and ink, watercolor,
and a few colored pencils on Strathmore Bristol.

When Dads Don't Grow Up

MARJORIE BLAIN PARKER

with pictures by R.W. ALLEY

Dial Books for Young Readers
an imprint of Penguin Group (USA) Inc.

Some dads

just never grow up.

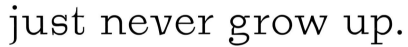

You can tell which ones they are.

They know that milk tastes better through a straw . . .

that bubble wrap is for popping . . .

and that rocks are for throwing (if there's water around).

Dads who haven't grown up still read the comics and watch cartoons.

They don't mind
sharing the couch
or checking for
monsters in closets.

And they love to mix up the words in bedtime stories.

Their kids are lucky.

When dads don't grow up

they understand
that shopping carts
are for racing . . .

that clothes don't
have to match . . .

and that pancakes
weren't meant
to be round.

They like to spend
a lot of time outside . . .

in sunshine,

rain,

or snow.

But they believe
in indoor sports, too.

So they're pretty good
at fixing things.

You know who they are.

They're the dads who aren't worried about looking goofy

or getting their hair wet
(if they still have any);

the ones who pretend they like
going out for fancy dinners,

when they'd rather
eat in the truck.

Dads who never grew up
really remember
what it's like
to be little:
    that mornings
    start *early* . . .

that basements
can be scary . . .

and that sitting still
is almost impossible.

They *never* stop trying to join in, either.

And sometimes they just forget how big they are.

(But usually that
comes in handy.)

Don't be fooled. They may look
like grown-ups on the outside,

but underneath they're just like us . . .

KIDS!